AF270638

US Space Force

by Julie Murray

Dash!
LEVELED READERS
An Imprint of Abdo Zoom • abdobooks.com

3

Level 1 – Beginning
Short and simple sentences with familiar words or patterns for children who are beginning to understand how letters and sounds go together.

Level 2 – Emerging
Longer words and sentences with more complex language patterns for readers who are practicing common words and letter sounds.

Level 3 – Transitional
More developed language and vocabulary for readers who are becoming more independent.

abdobooks.com

Published by Abdo Zoom, a division of ABDO, PO Box 398166, Minneapolis, Minnesota 55439. Copyright © 2022 by Abdo Consulting Group, Inc. International copyrights reserved in all countries. No part of this book may be reproduced in any form without written permission from the publisher. Dash!™ is a trademark and logo of Abdo Zoom.

Printed in the United States of America, North Mankato, Minnesota.
052021
092021

Photo Credits: iStock, US Air Force, US Space Force
Production Contributors: Kenny Abdo, Jennie Forsberg, Grace Hansen, John Hansen
Design Contributors: Candice Keimig, Neil Klinepier, Victoria Bates

Library of Congress Control Number: 2020919472

Publisher's Cataloging in Publication Data

Names: Murray, Julie, author.
Title: US Space Force / by Julie Murray
Description: Minneapolis, Minnesota : Abdo Zoom, 2022 | Series: Stellar space | Includes online resources and index.
Identifiers: ISBN 9781098226305 (lib. bdg.) | ISBN 9781098226442 (ebook) | ISBN 9781098226510 (Read-to-Me ebook)
Subjects: LCSH: Outer space--Juvenile literature. | United States. Department of the Air Force. Space Division--Juvenile literature. | Space control (Military science)--Juvenile literature. | United States. Air Force--History--Juvenile literature. | Astronautics--Juvenile literature.
Classification: DDC 358.8--dc23

Table of Contents

The Beginning 4

Missions 14

The Future 18

US Space Force Facts 22

Glossary 23

Index 24

Online Resources 24

The Beginning

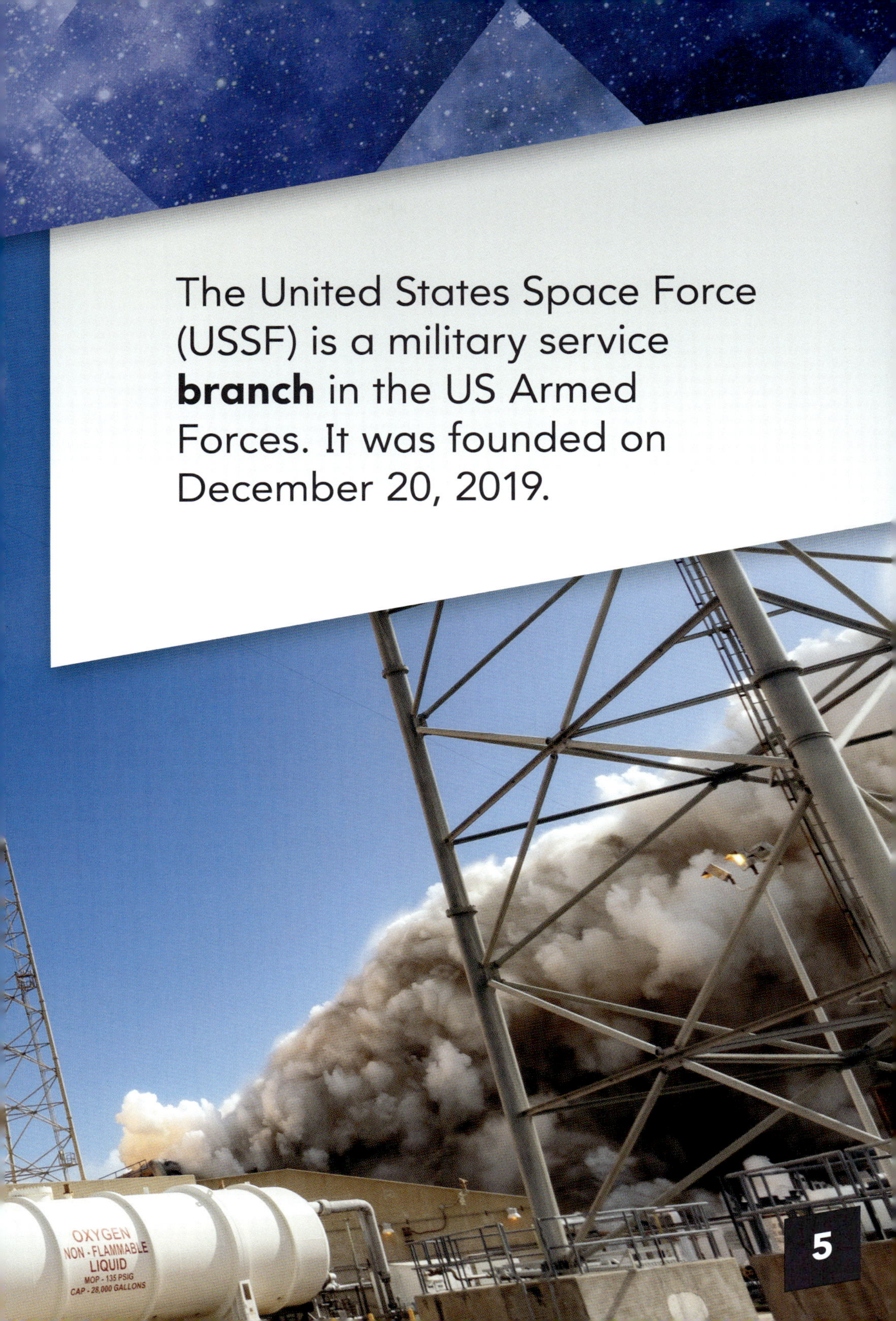

The United States Space Force (USSF) is a military service **branch** in the US Armed Forces. It was founded on December 20, 2019.

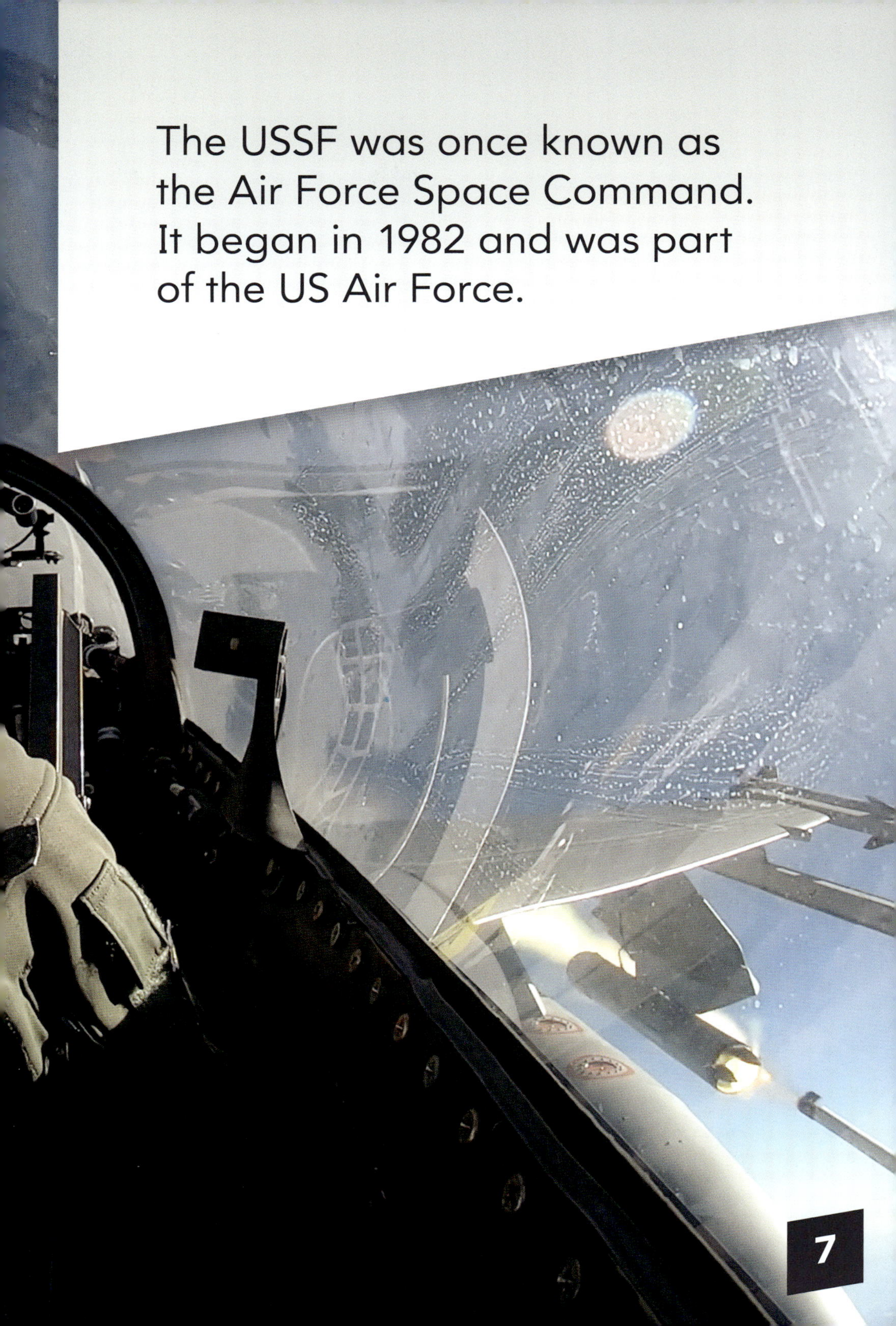

The USSF was once known as the Air Force Space Command. It began in 1982 and was part of the US Air Force.

The USSF's mission is to protect US interests in space. This includes everything from **satellites** that guide missiles to fighting **cyber warfare**.

10
RAYMOND
U.S.
UNITED STATE
SPACE COMMAN

The Chief of Space Operations (CSO) is the top military leader in the Space Force. This person is appointed by the president.

The first people to directly enlist in the Space Force graduated from basic training in December 2020. After technical training, they will begin their careers in the Space Force.

Missions
ULA

The US Space Force's first launch was on March 26, 2020. A communications **satellite** was sent into space. It will provide communications to US soldiers around the world.

Space Force has teamed up with SpaceX to launch Global Positioning **Satellites** (GPS). Space Force is also teaming up with NASA.

The two will work together in space policy, transportation, and spaceflight.

The Future

The first two Space Force locations were named in December 2020. Cape Canaveral Space Force Station and Patrick Space Force Base are located in Florida.

X-37B
ORBITAL TEST VEHICLE
ATLAS
ULA
United Launch Alliance

Space Force will evolve as we learn more about space every day. This stellar military **branch** even hopes to build a base on the moon!

US Space Force Facts

- Established as a military branch under the 2020 National Defense Authorization Act

- 16,000 personnel assigned to the branch

- Most of the first USSF members were assigned or transferred from the US Air Force

- General John W. Raymond became the branch's first CSO in 2019

- First launch took off from Cape Canaveral Air Force Station in Florida

- Operations budget in 2021 is $15.4 billion

Glossary

branch – a part of or a division of a larger organization.

cyber warfare – the use of computer technology to disrupt the activities of a state or organization, especially the deliberate attacking of information systems for strategic or military purposes.

satellite – a spacecraft that is sent into orbit around a planet or other heavenly body in order to collect information.

Index

Air Force 7

Cape Canaveral
Space Force 18

Chief of Space
Operations 11

Florida 18

goals 8, 21

launches 15, 16

mission 8

moon 21

NASA 16

Patrick Space Force
Base 18

SpaceX 16

training 13

US Armed Services 5

Online Resources

Booklinks
NONFICTION NETWORK
FREE! ONLINE NONFICTION RESOURCES

To learn more about the US Space Force, please visit **abdobooklinks.com** or scan this QR code. These links are routinely monitored and updated to provide the most current information available.